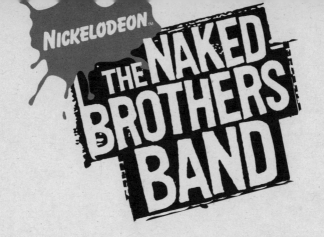

CRY WOLFF

Adapted by Michael Anthony Steele
Based on "VMAs" and "Wolff Brothers Cry Wolf"
written by Polly Draper

Based on *The Naked Brothers Band* created by Polly Draper

D0123219

SCHOLASTIC INC.

New York   Toronto   London   Auckland   Sydney
Mexico City   New Delhi   Hong Kong   Buenos Aires

ISBN-10: 0-545-03838-3
ISBN-13: 978-0-545-03838-6

Published by Scholastic Inc.
SCHOLASTIC and associated logos are trademarks and/or registered trademarks of Scholastic Inc.

12 11 10 9 8 7 6 5 4 3 2   8 9 10/0

Printed in the U.S.A.
First printing, January 2008

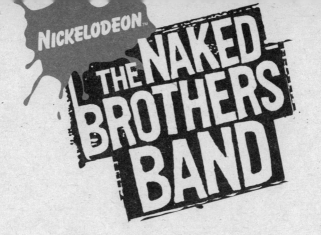

CRY WOLFF

Nat's fingers danced across the black and white keys of his electronic keyboard. He glanced up at the faces of his adoring fans. Although he was playing in a huge stadium, he could clearly make out the smiling faces of the people in the first few rows.

Nat looked back to see his brother Alex, playing drums. The rest of Nat's friends were in his band too. Thomas played cello, Qaasim played guitar, David played auxiliary keyboard, and Rosalina played bass guitar. Nat smiled. He was in a rock and roll band with all his best friends — and he was the lead singer. The crowd cheered as he sang one of his songs.

> *Cut up the banana*
> *Put it in a blender*
> *And shake it all up*
> *Shake it all up*

You've got a banana smoothie
You've got a banana smoothie

Nat's smile vanished as he opened his eyes. He was no longer in a packed stadium. He lay in a bunk bed just above his brother. There was no spotlight, no stadium, no screaming fans. It had all been a dream. But it was an awesome dream!

Then Nat listened to the song playing on the clock radio.

Shake it all up
You've got a banana smoothie
You've got a banana smoothie

Wait a minute. That *was* his song.

"Good morning, New York City," said the radio DJ. "This is Ryan Seacrest from Radio 640 where the hits never stop. That was, of course, the song "Banana Smoothie" written by the incredible Nat Wolff."

Oh, yeah! thought Nat. Even though it had all been a dream, he really *was* a rock star! He may have only been eleven, but he was the front man for the world-famous Naked Brothers Band.

Nat sat up, yawned, and swung his legs over the side of the bed. "Yes, you're absolutely right," he told the radio. "Nat *is* a genius."

"You're absolutely right," muttered a voice below. "Nat is an idiot."

Nat leaned over and scowled at his little brother, Alex. The younger boy's face was scrunched up against his pillow. His dark curly hair was well on its way to receiving the bed head of the year award. Alex gave Nat a devious smile.

Nat grabbed a fistful of pillow and was about to swat him when Ryan Seacrest's voice continued. "And his brother Alex, wow!" said the DJ.

"Yes!" shouted Alex. He sat up. "He's talking about me now!"

"Have you seen the way he plays those drums?" asked Seacrest.

"Say I'm a genius," Alex ordered.

"He's a little genius," said the DJ.

Nat chuckled. "A *little* genius."

Alex fell back onto his pillow. "Why am I a little everything?"

"How old is he now?" asked Seacrest. "Six? Seven?"

"I'm eight!" Alex screamed.

"He's just a baby," said the DJ. "I know that."

Nat leaped off the top bunk and descended on Alex. "A baby! A little teeny baby!" He began to tickle Alex's ribs. "Aww, look at him, he's so cute!"

Alex squirmed as he laughed uncontrollably. "Cut it out!" he shouted between cackles. "Don't tickle me!"

"I believe the Naked Brothers Band is nominated for an award tonight at the MTV Video Music Awards," said the DJ.

"Hey," said Nat. "They're talking about the awards tonight."

"I wish them luck," the DJ continued.

Alex threw Nat off and leaped out of bed. "Turn it off!" He dashed to the clock radio and banged on its buttons.

"But there's a lot of competition this year and . . ." said Seacrest before the radio went dead.

"Aw, poopoosauce," growled Alex. "I didn't get to it in time!"

Nat swung his legs off the bed. "Get to what in time?"

Alex groaned. "It ended on a bad sentence. If I'd turned it off before, it would have ended on a good sentence!"

"What are you talking about?" asked Nat.

"First, he wished us luck," explained Alex. "If I'd turned it off right away, it would have been a good sentence. But then Ryan Seacrest said *there's a lot of competition this year*. That made it a bad sentence!"

"Oh I get it," said Nat. He climbed out of bed.

"I turned it off on a bad sentence," said Alex. "Now we're going to lose!"

"Then I'll just turn it back on." Nat switched on the radio.

Again, Seacrest's voice came from the speakers. "Green Day has a great video this year. They might win."

"Noooooo!" yelled Alex.

Nat turned it off again.

"Ahh!" screamed Alex. He hopped with frustration. "Even worse! You just doubled our bad luck! Turn it back on!"

"But what if it's worse?" asked Nat. "Now you've got *me* scared."

"Just do it!" yelled Alex.

Nat slammed a hand onto the switch. "I'm a little concerned . . ." said the DJ's voice. Nat turned off the radio and Alex screamed again. Then Nat panicked and turned the radio on and off, on and off. Ryan Seacrest's voice stuttered from the stereo in negative segments. "I don't know . . . bad call . . . unfortunate . . ."

Finally, Nat left it on long enough for Ryan to get out a full sentence "Well, the Naked Brothers Band is my pick."

"Turn it off! Now!" yelled Alex.

Nat pushed the button again but nothing happened. He must have jammed it while banging on it.

"I'm sure they're going to win," Ryan added.

"Come on!" yelled Alex.

The pressure was too much. Nat picked up the small clock radio and threw it to the ground. It smashed open, spraying tiny electronic parts across the floor. But at least it had turned off.

"Yes, we did it!" Alex yelled as he danced around the room.

"Two good sentences!" said Nat. "Give me some fives!" The two brothers high-fived one another.

"That was a close one," said Alex.

Nat looked up and noticed that Mohammed was in their bedroom. He stood in the corner and aimed a large video camera lens at the two boys. Mohammed was one of the two cameramen who had followed them around two summers ago. He and another cameraman named Ken shot all the footage for the Naked Brothers Band documentary. Nat had forgotten that today was the first day of shooting for their newest project — a Naked Brothers Band TV series. Once again, cameras would videotape every aspect of their lives.

"Hey, Alex." Nat said, pointing to Mohammed. "Look who's here."

Alex's eyes widened. "Oh, no!" He reached down and grabbed a bowling pin, the first thing he could reach, to try and shield himself from the camera. "I'm wearing my smiley face boxers!" he screamed as he held the pin in front of him and shuffled behind some curtains. Nat burst into laughter.

While Alex took his turn in the shower, Nat went downstairs and made a breakfast of bacon, eggs, and toast for him and his brother. Ken and Mohammed followed him around with their cameras, videotaping everything he did.

Nat had long gotten used to living with cameras. Their first documentary was about how the Naked Brothers Band had formed and some of the troubles they went through. This new series would continue the story and show everyone what it was like being a rock star. Even though they never really said much, Ken and Mohammed had grown to be fixtures in Nat's and Alex's lives.

Alex yawned as he stepped down the purple spiral staircase. He wore his usual attire: shorts, a tank top, and a red, white, and blue bandanna on his head. He grabbed the plate of food Nat had made for him and carried it out of the kitchen.

Nat took his plate and sat down at the bar in the living room. The bright-orange room had a funky and fun rock-star vibe. Publicity stills hung on the walls, a colorful jukebox kicked out the jams, and a large egg-shaped chair made a cozy and cool-looking seat. They even had a basketball hoop for a quick pick-up game.

As Nat began eating, Alex shuffled through the room and back into the kitchen. He poured himself a glass of milk and grabbed a jar of peanut butter and a spoon. He sat at the bar next to Nat.

After a few bites, Nat looked into one of the cameras and began to speak. "Hi, I'm Nat Wolff."

"I'm Alex Wolff," said Alex with a mouthful of peanut butter.

"And we're just here calmly eating our breakfast with cameras in our house," Nat continued. "Even though today is the day of the big VMAs."

"Yep," agreed Alex. "Here I am. Eating peanut butter on a spoon and a nice tasty glass of milk." He took a long sip of milk. "My favorite breakfast."

Nat glanced at Alex's odd meal. "What about the eggs I made for you?"

Alex swallowed another clump of peanut butter. "No offense, but I gave them to Dad."

"Why did you give them to Dad?" asked Nat.

"He looked hungry," Alex replied. "I thought he should be fed."

Nat and Alex's dad walked down the stairs with an empty plate. He wore his blue penguin-covered pajamas. "Yummy eggs, Alex." He set his plate on the bar. "That was extremely thoughtful of you to make them for me."

Nat almost choked on a piece of toast. "Wait a minute!"

Mr. Wolff's eyes lit up as he spotted Ken and Mohammed. "Hey! Cameras!" He walked between the kids and the cameramen. A wide grin spread across his face. "Don't worry. We're used to having cameras in the house! I'm very comfortable in front of cameras. I just carry on as if they're not even there. I'm very natural." His smile disappeared and he glanced around. He pointed to his short brown hair. "I have a bit of a bald spot in the back, though. Could you just not . . ."

"Get a shot of the bald spot," Ken whispered to Mohammed.

As Mohammed moved the camera closer, Mr. Wolff covered his head. "No wait, I'll just be sure I'm facing front all the time." As both cameramen closed in, Mr. Wolff backed up the stairs. "Back. Back!" he yelled. He finally disappeared upstairs. The cameras turned back to Nat and Alex.

"I can't believe you took credit for those eggs," said Nat.

"I wanted to do a good deed for Dad," explained Alex.

"But that was my good deed," said Nat. "You stole my good deed."

Alex smiled. "I didn't steal it. I just re-gifted it."

Nat sighed and turned on the small television set on the bar. A bald guy stared back at them. "Oh look," said Nat. "It's Matt Pinfield."

Matt Pinfield was a TV host who followed the music scene. He knew almost everything there was to know about music — who was hot, who was not, who was on their way in, and who was on their way out.

"Turn it up," said Alex.

Nat turned up the volume. "Hi, I'm Matt Pinfield," the man said. "Today at three, I'll be giving my predictions for who is going to win the VMAs. So be sure and tune in." He gave a devious grin. "I'm never wrong."

Nat switched off the TV. "That makes me nervous."

"Me too," agreed Alex.

"It's an honor just to be nominated, right?" asked Nat.

"Yeah," said Alex. "But I really want to win."

Nat nodded. "Me too."

Suddenly, accordion music blared through the room. Their dad stepped off the stairs and stared into the nearest video camera. He had put on a hat to cover his bald spot.

"Hi, I'm just playing my accordion," he said, speaking over the loud music. "Don't mind me."

Nat rolled his eyes as Alex's head dropped to the counter.

Mr. Wolff sidled up to the boys. "I was wondering if you were going to need me to sit in tonight when you play at the awards."

"No!" Alex said without looking up.

Nat smiled, trying not to hurt his dad's feeling. "No thanks, Dad. We're fine."

"No worries," said Mr. Wolff. "But I'll bring my accordion in case you change your mind."

"We won't," said Alex.

"No worries," said Mr. Wolff. Still playing, he strolled out of the room.

Alex raised his head and glared at his brother. "Don't cave, Nat."

"I won't," whispered Nat.

Their dad always tried to get in on their rock-star lives. He was a musician as well, but he mainly performed in plays and at German restaurants. He was a great father, and Nat sometimes let him do things with the band. Nat felt guilty and wondered if tonight should be one of those times.

As if reading his mind, Alex squinted at his brother. "Be strong," he said through clenched teeth.

Nat sighed. "I know."

Later that morning, Nat and Alex played a quick game of basketball with the hoop in their living room. They tried to relax and not worry about winning that night. So far, it wasn't working.

Cooper entered the apartment. Dressed in his usual suit, tie, and large-rimmed glasses, he spoke on his cell phone. "Now, make sure the limo isn't late," he instructed. "This is the most important day of our lives."

Cooper had been the Naked Brothers Band's manager from the very beginning, back when they were called the Silver Boulders. He was a shrewd negotiator and always got the best deals for them. And even though he was only eleven, he took care of the band as well as any grown-up.

Cooper set down his briefcase and grabbed the bouncing basketball after Alex made a shot. "I got the rundown for tonight," he said. "You sing 'I'm Out' and then, at about nine, the best rock award will be announced." He shot the ball and made a basket.

Nat grabbed the bouncing ball. "Do you think we have a chance?" he asked. "It's the first time we've ever been nominated for something. I really want to win." His shot bounced off the rim of the basket.

"I know," said Cooper. "But there's a lot of competition this year."

Alex caught the ball. "Don't say that!"

"Yeah, why does everyone say that?" asked Nat.

"I think we have a good chance though," said Cooper.

"Man, you scared me," said Alex. He tossed the ball through the hoop. "You almost ended it on a bad note."

As Nat grabbed the ball, Jesse entered the apartment. Jesse was their babysitter and tutor. Her long brown hair was pulled into a ponytail. She had almost as many tattoos as Alex; Jesse's were real though.

"You guys, you won't believe how I got here this morning," she squealed.

"How?" asked Alex.

Jesse set down her bag and trotted over to the window. "Look outside."

Nat opened the window and the four of them jutted

their heads outside. Three stories below, parked in the street, was a man sitting on the strangest bicycle Nat had ever seen. Where the handlebars would be on a normal bike, there was a circle of six seats, pedals, and handlebars.

"Cool! What is it?" asked Nat.

"It's a bicycle built for six," replied Jesse. "This guy, George, gave me a ride." George waved up at Jesse and yelled something in a foreign language.

Alex pulled his head inside angrily. "You took a ride with a strange man?"

Jesse shrugged. "It was free."

"Free?" growled Alex. "I don't think so. Not with a guy named George."

Jesse reached over and squeezed Alex's cheek with one hand. "Alex, you're such a little sweetie. You're always worried about me."

Alex smiled up at her. "No need for the 'little.' Plain old sweetie will do. Or even darling."

Jesse smiled and patted him on the head. As she walked over to her purse, Alex looked into Ken's video camera and boasted, "She's still crazy about me. Even after all these years."

Even though Jesse was in her twenties and Alex was only eight, he believed she was his girlfriend. She playfully called him her *little* boyfriend but still dated other guys her own age. That always bothered Alex, but he hoped she would come around someday.

"Hey, Nat, I brought you your horoscope for today," said Jesse. She dug through her purse. "It's totally meant for you. Want to hear it?"

"Sure," said Nat.

Cooper and Alex continued to shoot hoops while Jesse pulled out a newspaper. She flipped it open and began to read. "All responsibility falls on you today. You will succeed only if you accept today's challenges. If you don't, you'll take everyone down with you."

Nat's mouth fell open. "Wow, no pressure on me," he said sarcastically. "Thanks for reading that to me, Jess."

"No problem!" she said with a smile, not picking up on his sarcasm at all. "Isn't that so right-on that it gives you the chills?"

"It definitely gives me the chills," Nat agreed.

"Are those horoscopes accurate?" asked Cooper.

"Oh, my gosh, they're so accurate it's scary!" said Jesse. "Once, my friend had this horoscope that said he would get food poisoning that day and he *totally* did."

"What happened to him?" asked Cooper.

"He died," replied Jesse. "And all because of Clam's Casino."

"And his horoscope predicted it?" asked Nat.

Jesse nodded. "I'm afraid so."

Cooper and Alex stopped playing. "What's mine say?" asked Cooper.

"Yeah, tell me mine, too," said Alex.

"Cooper, you're January, let's see . . . ." She ran a finger down the page. Everyone gathered around her. "You normally like to use brains over brawn but today is opposite day for you," she read. "If you want today to go smoothly, don't be afraid of resorting to a little violence." Jesse looked up and smiled. "Cool! You can totally Jackie Chan–out today, Cooper!"

Cooper grinned. "Cool."

"What's mine?" asked Alex.

Jesse scanned the page then quickly covered it with both hands. "Oopsies, never mind. We don't have to read yours."

Alex's eyes widened. "Why not?"

"Because . . . um . . . it's kind of a downer," she replied.

"As opposed to mine, which was really uplifting?" asked Nat.

Jesse looked at Nat with wide eyes. "This one is way worse."

"Well, now you *have* to tell him," said Cooper.

"Yeah," agreed Alex. "I have to be prepared!"

Jesse sighed and held up the paper. "There's no way around it. Today is *not* your lucky day," she read. "Try not to get out of bed. And if you absolutely must, stay away from motor vehicles and falling objects."

She put the paper down and looked at Alex. Everyone looked at him but he didn't say anything. He simply stared at the paper. Nat was surprised. He took that better than expected.

"Aaaaaaaaaah!" screamed Alex. He shot up and ran to the stairs.

Then again, maybe not, thought Nat.

Nat found Alex in their bedroom, sitting in bed with his back against the wall. The blanket was pulled up to his chin. Nat sat beside him.

"Dude, it's just a horoscope," Nat reassured him. "I'm sure it's not true."

"Yeah, I'm sure the Clam's Casino guy said the same thing before he bit the dust," said Alex. He leaned his head on Nat's shoulder. "I just want you to know that if I die today, I'm sorry I didn't eat your eggs."

"Alex, you're not going to die today," said Nat. He put a hand on his shoulder. "I'm going to watch over you really carefully."

Alex sat up and threw Nat's arm off. "What good is that? You'll just fail and bring everyone down with you like your horoscope says."

"Just please get out of bed," Nat pleaded. "The band will be here any minute."

"All right," said Alex. He slowly climbed down. "But if anything falls on me and kills me, my death is on your head."

Nat hopped down and grabbed a large fish pillow and a jump rope. "Here . . ." He placed the pillow on Alex's head and tied it down by looping the jump rope under his chin. "Now if anything falls on your head, you'll be fine."

Alex glared up at him from under the big fish. Nat had to bite his tongue to keep from laughing. "What about the motor vehicles situation?" asked Alex. "What are we going to do about that?"

"Let's cross that bridge when we come to it," replied Nat.

"Are you crazy?" Alex threw off the fish pillow. "I'm not crossing any bridges today!" He jumped back into bed and began beating the mattress with his fists. "We're going to lose! We're going to lose! Our first time nominated for an award, and we're going to lose!"

"Alex, stop!" shouted Nat.

His little brother yelled into his pillow. "Matt Pinfield's going to predict we're going to lose, and he's never wrong. We're going to lose! I can feel it! We're going to lose, and I'm going to die from a motor vehicle!"

"Stop it, right now!" ordered Nat. "Don't end it on a bad note."

Alex stopped and looked up. "Oh, yeah." He stood up and began to hop up and down. "We're going to win! We're going to win! I'm going to live!"

Nat left Alex in their bedroom to calm down. As he descended the staircase, Thomas, David, and Qaasim arrived. Thomas dragged in his cello case while Qaasim carried his electric guitar case. David brought along his short, chubby Boston terrier, E.T. They set down their gear and went right up to Ken's camera.

"Hi," said Thomas, waving to the camera. "We're the Naked Brothers Band." The tallest of the group, his short brown hair poked out from beneath his hat. He also wore his usual mischievous smile. "I'm Thomas and this is David." He pointed to the shorter blond-haired boy beside him.

"And this is my dog, E.T." David added. He held up the smushed-nosed black and white dog. "He's our mascot."

"Who just peed in the hallway," added Thomas. The boys laughed. Thomas reached over and pulled Qaasim into the camera's view.

Qaasim waved. "And I'm Qaasim, the new guy." His long dreadlocks were pulled back under a black cap.

"Qaasim Asani Malik Middleton," added Thomas.

"Yeah, Qaasim took Josh's place," said David. Josh was their former lead guitarist.

"He's a genius," said Thomas. "Say something smart, Qaasim."

"Something smart, Qaasim," joked Qaasim. He gave the camera one more grin before walking up to Jesse. "Hey, Jesse, there's a guy downstairs on some crazy bicycle. He says he's waiting for you."

"Oh no!" Jesse put down her magazine and ran to the window. "I told him to go away."

Thomas plopped down on the couch. "Hey Jesse, we want to look real sharp when we win the award tonight. Can you do our hair?"

"Sure," Jesse replied. Then she opened the window and leaned out. "Bye-bye, George!" She waved. "You have to go now." George's shouting could be heard all the way up on the third floor. However, no one could understand what he was saying.

Jesse looked back at the others. "Does anyone know how to say bye-bye in Romanian or Mediterranean or any of the -anian languages?"

Alex stomped down the stairs with the fish pillow on his head.

David chuckled. "Alex, why do you have a pillow tied to your head?"

"My horoscope says I have to beware of falling objects," he replied.

Thomas pointed to the ceiling. "Alex, look out!"

Alex ducked and glanced around. "What? Where?!"

"There! There!" shouted David, pointing to a light. "That light's going to fall on you!"

Qaasim sighed, "They're just messing with your head, man."

Alex growled, "You guys are such wimps."

"Does anyone know where Rosalina is?" asked Nat.

"You mean your *true love*?" asked Thomas. He and David began making kissing sounds. Nat just rolled his eyes.

"Yeah, where is the lovely and talented Rosalina?" asked Qaasim.

Nat sighed. "Qaasim, you aren't going to tease me about her, too, are you?"

"*Au contraire*, my dude," Qaasim replied. "I commend you for your taste in women."

"Ooh, Qaasim's going to steal her away from you, Nat," said David.

Nat frowned. "There's nothing to steal. She doesn't like me anyway." Nat hoped that wasn't true. Even though she was two years older, Nat had a not-so-secret crush on Rosalina.

"I'd never steal another man's woman," declared Qaasim.

"She's not my *woman*!" said Nat.

"Right," agreed Thomas. "She's his *hamster*."

"Maybe she's his *bookcase*," suggested David.

Thomas pointed to the ceiling. "Hey Alex, look out! Falling object!"

Alex covered his head. "Where?"

"Man, these fools are pranking you!" said Qaaism. "Stop falling for their baloney and ham on rye!"

"How old are you guys anyway?" asked Nat. "Like five?"

"Hey, Nat," said David. "Your pants are falling down."

Nat rolled his eyes. "Yeah, right." He wasn't falling for that old gag.

Qaasim pointed to Nat's feet. "No, man, they really are."

Nat looked down and saw that his pants now sat crumpled around his ankles. He quickly pulled them up over his boxer shorts. "I like them a little large," he explained.

David and Thomas burst into laughter.

Cooper stepped in the middle and held out his hands. "I think we should just start rehearsing without Rosalina. She's getting her braces off today, and I think it takes a while."

Jesse walked away from the window and sat back on the couch. "Just let me know when you guys want me to do your hair for you."

"Sweet!" said Thomas. He glanced at Alex then whispered something into David's ear. The two ducked into the practice room.

Qaasim unzipped his guitar case and reached a hand inside. "Actually, I brought my own with me." He pulled out a fuzzy afro wig.

"What is that thing?" asked Alex.

"It's a Jimi Hendrix wig," Qaasim replied.

Nat noticed lots of tiny white specks tangled in the curly hair. "It doesn't look Jimi Hendrix–ish."

"I know," said Qaasim. He began plucking out the white bits. "My mom accidentally put it in the wash."

"Why is there white stuff in it?" asked Alex.

"Oh that's just lint," replied Qaasim. "She washed it with the socks."

Nat laughed and shook his head. "Okay, guys, let's rehearse the song for tonight."

Qaasim pulled out his guitar and he, Nat, and Alex went into the practice room. David and Thomas were already there. David sat at the piano while Thomas stood to the side with his cello. Nat became very suspicious. It wasn't like them to be so eager to practice.

Qaasim plugged in his guitar while Alex grabbed his drumsticks and sat behind the drum set. David played a note on the piano, and Thomas and Qaasim tuned their instruments.

When he finished tuning his cello, Thomas turned to Alex. "Dude, you can't drum with that pillow on your head."

"Yeah," agreed David. "Take it off. Nothing's going to happen to you."

"Don't be a baby," Thomas teased.

"I'm not a baby, you numchucks." Alex ripped the pillow away and threw it to the floor. "See? It's off."

Thomas snickered. "Aren't you scared of falling objects?"

"No," replied Alex. "I'm just ware."

"What does *ware* mean?" asked Nat.

"Ware," Alex repeated. "My fortune said *be ware*. I'm being ware." Alex twirled a drumstick with one hand and began to warm up. He played a quick riff on the hi-hat while keeping time with the pounding bass drum.

Suddenly, Thomas zipped across the room to a rope dangling down the wall. Nat followed the rope as it ran up the wall, across the ceiling, and to a bucket of water perched over Alex's head. Before Nat could say anything, Thomas yanked it. The bucket dumped water all over Alex. Nat couldn't help but laugh as his little brother totally freaked out.

"Aaaaaaaaaaaaaahh!" screamed Alex. Thomas and David cracked up and dashed out of the room. Alex hopped up and chased after them. "I hate you guys!"

"Come on out, Alex." Nat pounded on the bathroom door. Alex had locked himself in there for over half an hour. "We need to rehearse."

Nat sighed and turned to Ken's camera. "Everybody's tense about the awards tonight so they're doing crazy things. We all usually get along really well."

Jesse squeezed past the camera and knocked on the bathroom door. "Alex, sweetie. I need to get in there. I need some hair goo for the guys' hairstyles."

Alex opened the door and stepped out.

"Oh, Alex, are you feeling better?" she asked, giving him a great big hug.

"Yeah," he replied. He handed her a small round container. "Here's some hair goo for the hairstyles," he said innocently.

"You are such a sweetie," said Jesse.

Alex smiled. "Forgive and forget, that's my motto."

After Jesse walked away, Alex turned to face the camera. "It's not hair goo," he confessed with a devilish smile. "It's Hot Ice Vapor Rub." He rubbed his palms together wickedly. "It's payback time."

Alex joined the rest of the band in the polka-dot room. The round room had white walls, which had giant red polka dots painted on them, and sunlight poured in through huge circular windows. The floor was covered with yellow shag carpet. The Wolff brothers and their friends could sit on any number of blue inflatable couches and chairs or on the tall, carpet-covered bench that lined the room. As they went inside, Thomas and David thumbed through one of Jesse's hair books while Qaasim sat by himself, picking lint out of his wig.

Thomas pointed to the book. "Can I have this hairstyle?"

"The Big Kahuna?" asked Jesse. "Okay, I'll see what I can do." She dipped her hand into the can of goo and slapped a wad onto Thomas's head.

David pointed to another picture. "What about this one for me? The Porcupine."

"Okay," replied Jesse. She slapped a wad of goo onto David's head as well.

Jesse quickly molded Thomas's hair into a tall pompadour. The rounded hairstyle jutted up and over his forehead like an exaggerated hairstyle from the 50s. Meanwhile, she formed David's hair into several large spikes. He looked like a punk-rock porcupine. Alex sat behind them with his hands over his mouth. He could hardly contain himself.

David reached up and touched his spiky hair. "This feels kind of tingly."

"Really?" asked Jesse. She used some more goo to form another long spike. "Because hair goo is only made with . . . goo stuff."

Thomas put both hands onto his hair. "Yeah, my head feels . . . spicy."

David clawed at his hair. "My head is on fire! I'm not kidding!"

"Mine too!" yelled Thomas. He grabbed his head. "Help!"

Alex burst into laughter and pointed at Thomas and David. "I punked you punks!"

"We need water!" yelled David. He ran out of the room.

"Help us!" shouted Thomas as he followed.

Nat and Alex chased after them as they ran into the kitchen. They shoved their heads under the faucet as Thomas turned on the water. David pulled out the vegetable sprayer and began to hose himself down. Thomas yanked the sprayer from him and squirted his head as well. Alex continued to laugh.

Through all the screaming, Nat heard a faint knock. He ran to the front door and opened it to see Rosalina. Her long brown hair was in two braids draping over her shoulders. She peered inside to investigate the screaming.

"What's going on?" she asked, laughing lightly. Then she quickly had to step out of the way as Thomas and David plowed by, running through the doorway at full speed into the hallway.

"Our heads are on fire!" yelled Thomas.

"Help us!" screamed David.

Nat jumped out of the way as Alex chased after them. "I totally punked you suckers!" he yelled. "Now we're even!"

Then Jesse flew by, chasing after them, shouting, "You guys totally ruined my stylings! You can't pour water over the Big Kahuna!"

Then Cooper sprinted after them, screaming, "You guys have to rehearse!"

After everyone had ran out of the apartment like maniacs, Rosalina and Nat stayed glued to the door jams, just in case. Finally Qaasim ran through the hallway after the rest of the gang, "What about my Jimi Hendrix wig?" he howled.

Rosalina peered down the hallway to see if anyone else was coming. She stepped inside and Nat shut the door. "What's going on?" she asked again, more confused than ever.

Nat tried to act cool, "Everyone's just acting a little crazy because of the award show." Trying to pretend nothing happened, he casually turned and walked inside. Unfortunately, he slipped on a puddle of water and fell to the ground. So much for looking cool.

Nat and Rosalina waited in the kitchen for the others to return. He racked his brain trying to come up with things to say, but he always had a tough time talking to Rosalina.

Being the front man for the band, Nat had all of their girl fans screaming after him. That's how he got the nickname, "Girl Magnet." Unfortunately, his title didn't give him enough confidence to speak comfortably around Rosalina. Two summers ago, he was so nervous that he only spoke to her in a silly British accent. At least he didn't do that anymore.

Finally, Rosalina broke the ice. "You know, Matt Pinfield will be on in a few minutes with his predictions."

"Yeah, I'm nervous about that," he confessed.

Rosalina smiled. "Me too."

Suddenly, Nat felt a cool breeze around his legs. He didn't want to look down, but he had a feeling he knew what happened: His baggy pants probably fell down again.

He tried to act casual about it, hoping that somehow Rosalina wouldn't notice. "So, you got your braces off, I see," he said. "Sweet."

"Yeah," said Rosalina.

"They look really good," said Nat. "Yay, teeth!" He cringed inside. *What kind of idiot says "Yay, teeth"?*

Rosalina giggled. "Thanks."

Nat shook his head. There was another long awkward pause. He smiled. "So . . . how's it going?"

"Good," Rosalina replied. She glanced down. "Uh, Nat? Your pants fell down."

"Oh, right," said Nat casually. He quickly pulled them back up and tried to act like it happened all the time. Unfortunately, he felt his face warm as he blushed. He supposed it could have been worse. At least his boxers didn't have smiley faces on them like Alex's.

The rest of the band finally returned. David and Thomas had washed out their hair and put on hats to cover their ruined styles. Jesse got over being upset about her destroyed hair-dos and helped Qaasim with his wig. She pulled all the lint out and teased it to twice its normal size. Once the apartment was calm again (or as calm as the Wolff's apartment ever could be), everyone gathered around the TV in the living room. Matt Pinfield was just about to give his predictions for the VMAs.

Nat sighed. "Here we go."

He pushed a button on the remote, and Pinfield's familiar bald head filled the screen. "There's a lot of competition this year," were the first words out of his mouth.

"Don't say that," said Alex.

"A *lot* of competition," he repeated.

Alex groaned. "We heard you the first time, bub!"

"Yeah, I don't think the Naked Brothers Band is going to win it this year," Pinfield predicted.

Alex leaped to his feet. "Oh no! Turn it off! Turn it off!"

"I thought we had to wait for a good note," said Nat.

Alex sat back down. "Right! Keep it on! Keep it on!"

"The turnover in that band is harder to keep up with than Diddy's name changes," said Pinfield.

"What is he talking about?" asked Nat. "Bands break up and re-form all the time."

"They have some new guitar player in the band now," Pinfield continued.

"My name is Qaasim, fool!" yelled Qaasim.

"And how about those knuckleheads that left the band and then came back?" he asked.

37

"Hey!" yelled David. "Are we the knuckleheads he's talking about?"

Thomas shrugged. "It was only for a summer."

"I mean, Nat's got to be an idiot to take them back," Pinfield ranted. "Of course, when all he has is that soda-holic brother of his, I guess those other two look pretty good."

For a while there, Alex went on a lemon-lime soda binge. Since then, he'd switched over to milk. "I'm a milk-aholic now, you booger!" yelled Alex.

Cooper got to his feet and marched to the TV. "Hieeeee-ya!" he screeched as he slammed the set with two quick karate chops. The TV screen went dark. Cooper dusted off his hands. "Okay, it's off!"

Jesse clapped her hands. "Yay, Cooper!"

"Sorry," he apologized. "My horoscope said I was supposed to resort to physical violence today."

"No problem, man," said Nat, impressed.

Alex stood and walked toward the TV. "Sorry guys. I have to turn it back on. We have to wait for a good note." Alex smacked the set and Matt Pinfield came back on the screen. He continued to rant about their band.

"I mean, we know Nat only put Rosalina in the band because he has a crush on her," he said. "Who knows if she can even play an instrument?"

"She plays ten instruments, you moron!" Nat yelled at the screen.

Rosalina's jaw dropped. "He thinks I can't play," she said. "I don't believe this!"

"So, my prediction is . . ." Pinfield gave a dramatic pause. "The Naked Brothers Band is going down. Muah-hah-ha!" His face contorted grotesquely as he burst into maniacal laughter.

Nat clasped his brother's shoulder. "This guy isn't going to end it on a good note, Alex."

Just then, a large stage light fell from above Matt Pinfield and landed squarely on his head. His laughter was cut short as he grunted and fell out of frame.

Alex smiled and began hopping up and down excitedly. "It ended on a good note!" he yelled. "It ended on a good note!" Everyone else jumped around with him tossing pillows at each other.

By six o'clock, everyone was putting the finishing touches on their outfits. Rosalina painted a few hot pink streaks in her hair and wore a lacey ruffled skirt with boots. Qaasim wore a 60s outfit, complete with a fuzzy orange vest; it matched his Hendrix wig perfectly. Alex wore a powder blue suit with no sleeves, a big bowtie, and an oversized Uncle Sam hat.

David and Thomas came up with equally outrageous outfits to work with their hats. David wore a brown suit vest over a striped shirt. Thomas donned a brightly colored shirt in contrast to his simple knit cap. Of all of them, Nat was the most conservative. He wore a brown suit jacket with jeans that had one leg cut off at the knee.

Their music gear had already been sent over. They had a limousine waiting downstairs, and even Jesse had finished getting ready. Everything was on schedule.

As they finished, Mr. Wolff popped into the packed bedroom. "I just want you to know that I'm bringing my accordion tonight just in case you guys change your minds about letting me sit in."

"Whatever, Dad," said Nat.

His father's face brightened. "You mean *whatever* I get to sit in? Or *whatever* I'll have my accordion just in case? Or *whatever* . . ."

Cooper reached up and grabbed Mr. Wolff by the shirt. He shook him back and forth. "He just means *whatever*, okay?!" Cooper let go and regained his composure. "Sorry, Mr. Wolff. My horoscope said I should use a little violence today."

Mr. Wolff smiled. "No worries." He ducked out of the room. "I'll just go get my accordion."

As the group filed out of the bedroom, Rosalina grabbed Nat's arm. "Nat, you have to know that no matter what happens tonight, we're still the greatest band ever. And it's all because of you."

Everyone agreed.

"Thanks, you guys," said Nat. He didn't feel solely responsible for their success, but he was grateful for their appreciation.

Surprisingly, Nat didn't feel nervous anymore. The award no longer seemed like such a big deal. What really mattered was the great time he had with his family and friends. He looked over at their smiling faces. "Now let's go to that award ceremony and kick some butt!" he shouted.

"Yeah!" everyone yelled.

They marched downstairs and onto the sidewalk below. A long black limo was parked on the street in front of their apartment building. The limo driver opened the back door, and the band piled in.

Nat and Alex were the last to approach the car when Alex stopped dead in his tracks. "Hey! My horoscope says I shouldn't ride in a motor vehicle today!"

Cooper climbed out of the car and grabbed Alex's arm. "You have to, Alex."

Alex gave him a serious look. "A life is very precious thing to waste, man."

Jesse climbed out of the car. "Wait a minute," she said. "I have an idea." She waved to someone parked in front of the limo. It was George and his bicycle built for six.

The Naked Brothers Band rode to the Video Music Awards on George's bizarre peddling contraption, keeping in the tradition of outrageous rock-star behavior. Jesse, Cooper, Mr. Wolff, and the camera crew followed them in the limo.

Mr. Wolff stood and waved to the people of New York from the open sunroof.

When they pulled up in front of the red carpet, the fans went wild. They screamed, waved, and chanted "Naked Brothers Band! Naked Brothers Band!"

Nat thanked George as they climbed off the bike and strutted up the red carpet. Barricades held back hordes of adoring fans. Flashes from the cameras of reporters and paparazzi lit up the night. The band smiled and waved as they neared the entrance. Unfortunately, a familiar face greeted them by the door.

"Over here!" shouted Matt Pinfield. He and his own cameraman waved them over for an interview. Matt had an ice-pack strapped to his head, wore a neck brace, and had one arm in a sling. He held a cordless mike with his good hand. "I'm Matt Pinfield. Sorry for my appearance, a flying stage light hit me on the head earlier today. And I got in a little car accident on the way over here."

"Wait a minute," said Cooper. "Alex, what sign are you again?"

"Scorpio," Alex replied.

Cooper turned back to the man. "Are you by any chance a Scorpio?"

"Yes I am," Pinfield replied.

Everyone laughed. It turned out that all of the bad stuff ended up happening to Matt Pinfield instead of Alex.

But Matt Pinfield didn't get the joke. Instead, he shook Cooper's hand. "Great to see you, Cooper. Listen, are you guys pumped about tonight?"

"You think we're going down?" asked Cooper. "We think *you're* going down!" Cooper spun around and flipped Pinfield over his shoulder. "Hieeeee-ya!"

The rest of the band laughed as they stepped over Matt Pinfield on their way inside. Even E.T. hopped onto his chest as he followed David.

"I'll get you Naked Brothers Band!" he yelled. "And your little dog too!"

Once inside, Nat had a great time watching the awards ceremony. No longer nervous, he was able to have a great time with his friends. But when they read the winner for the best music video, the night got even better.

"And the award for best rock video goes to . . . the Naked Brothers Band!"

The band leaped up from their seats as the auditorium erupted in applause. Nat led the group as they made their way down the aisle and up the stage. Even Jesse, Mr. Wolff, and E.T. joined them.

Nat turned over the award in his hand. It was in the shape of a silver astronaut holding a flag — the MTV Moonman. Nat held it up and faced the audience. "We've been really nervous about this award show all day," he said into the microphone. "My horoscope said that if I failed I would take everyone down with me. But I now realize that when you have a great family and true friends, you can't fail. And what's important is not the award, but the love that went into making the music. Thank you!"

As the audience applauded, Nat and Alex's dad erupted into an accordion solo behind them.

"Hey, Dad!" yelled Alex. "Get off the stage!"

The next day, Nat was excited to get back to work. The band was filming their next music video, for "Sometimes I'll Be There." Trailed by Alex and the documentary cameramen, he met the band at their personal studio a few blocks away. The facility was set up for shooting videos as well as recording CDs. It had two large sound stages (large rooms used for video production) as well as a recording studio (a smaller soundproof room used for recording music). The facility also held several dressing rooms, offices, and even a kitchen.

When they arrived, Nat and Alex went to their dressing rooms and donned their costumes. This music video was going to have an Arabian motif. Nat had to dress as a genie, sporting silky baggy pants, a shiny shirt, and a vest. He topped it off with a silk turban.

Nat met Rosalina on the sound stage for a lighting check. The art department built a set that looked just like an Arabian tent in the desert. Colorful fabrics draped over-head, and large pillows covered the floor. A large tray of fruit was placed on a low table. Nat knew better than to try any though. Like most things on film sets, the fruit was probably fake. Real fruit would go bad under all the hot lights. The floor was covered with sand, and a mural of a desert scene hung behind them. From the camera's point of view, it would look as if they were in an ancient Arabic land.

Nat and Rosalina lay on the pillows while the crew adjusted the lights above. Rosalina was dressed as an Arabian princess. She wore a small hat with pink sheer scarves drap-ing under her chin. As they watched the technicians bustle about, Nat and Rosalina took the opportunity to talk to the documentary cameras.

Nat looked into Ken's camera and waved. "Hi!"

"Hi." Rosalina did the same.

"We're here on the set of the music video for our song called 'Sometimes I'll Be There,'" Nat explained.

"Nat's song is about a mysterious place in Arabia," Rosalina joked.

Nat laughed. "It is?" The song wasn't really about that. The director had merely decided to use the exotic location as a backdrop. Video directors were like that sometimes.

"The director thought Nat should be a genie trapped in a lamp," Rosalina explained. "And I am an Arabian princess who tries to rescue him."

"But I want her to live with me in my bottle and she wants me to live in her world," Nat added. "In the end we have to part."

She glanced at Nat. "It's really sad."

"Hey guys," said Alex as he walked onto the set. He wore a costume similar to Nat's, except his turban had a big peacock feather jutting out from the front. He immediately went for the tray of fake fruit.

"Alex, don't eat that," Nat warned.

It was too late. Alex popped a grape into his mouth. He made a sour face. "Oh, yuck! Cement grapes!" He spit out the fake grape and picked up the heavy bowl. He moved it closer to Ken's camera. "Hi, everybody. Would you like some lovely grapes?" he joked. "Just reach through your TV and grab them." Nat and Rosalina laughed as he pushed the grapes closer to the lens. Alex smiled. "Ah, you're too smart. You know they're fake."

"Alex, we're just telling them about the music video," said Nat.

Alex plopped down between Nat and Rosalina. "Oh yeah, I get to marry the Arabian princess."

"Against her will," Nat added.

"Yeah but still, I win her," said Alex.

"But she loves me," said Nat.

"Who cares? I win and you lose, buckaroonie." Not thinking, Alex popped another grape into his mouth. He immediately spit it out. "Oh man, I did it again." Nat and Rosalina laughed.

Once everything was ready to go, Nat and the others began to shoot. The rest of the band members were in costumes as well. However, they had a smaller part in the storytelling scenes where Nat and Alex fought over the princess. They did join in the scenes where the band actually performed the song. With their instruments set up in the fake tent, everyone pretended to play and sing as the speakers played back their pre-recorded song. As usual, they all had a great time playing around on the set.

After a full day of shooting, Nat and the others watched their last take on the video monitor. Cooper and the director sat in their usual spot just off the set, behind the cameras. The director was tall, thin, and had dark curly hair. He spoke with an accent that made him sound like Dracula.

Nat bobbed his head in time with the music as he watched a scene where everyone sang together. Then each played their instruments on the sand. The segment looked great. Nat knew their fans would love it.

The director leaned over to Cooper. "VMAs are okay. But this video is the one I win my Obelisk for."

"What's an Obelisk?" asked Cooper.

The director beamed. "It is most important award in my country for music videos."

"What country are you from again?" asked Nat.

The director turned and gave Nat a sly smile. "Don't you know?"

"The country where they bite necks?" asked Qaasim.

"Yes," he replied. His grin widened.

"And suck blood?" asked Thomas.

"Yes," he repeated.

"And give Obelisks for cool music videos?" asked Cooper.

"Exactly, Super Cooper!" He gave Cooper a high five with an added elbow bump.

"Cool," said Cooper.

As the song came to the end, the director stood. He pointed to the screen. "Okay, here comes the falling shot, right here."

On the screen, Nat fell away from his keyboard and onto the sand. The camera zoomed in on his face.

"And then, to win the Obelisk," said the director, "we have a crying shot, right here. With real tears!" The screen went black and the words "Close Up Crying Shot" appeared.

Nat felt a little queasy. He didn't know he'd have to have to cry on camera. He'd never done that before. "Real tears?" asked Nat.

The director turned to him and smiled. "Real tears."

Nat swallowed hard. He hoped he could pull it off.

Back at the apartment, Nat stood in front of the bathroom mirror. His face was twisted in agony as he sobbed loudly.

Alex poked his head in. "What are you doing?"

Nat relaxed his face. "I'm trying to fake cry. The director wants me to do it at the end of the video." Nat contorted his face once more. He squeezed out another loud cry.

Alex cocked his head. "No offense, but it kind of looks like you're laughing."

Nat stopped. "It does?"

"Yeah, you're squinching your face up in sort of a smiley way," he replied.

"I bet you can't do it," said Nat.

"Yes I can," replied Alex. "But do you want to see something first?"

"What?" asked Nat.

"I finally perfected my smile." Alex leaned closer to the mirror. He gave a small grin. "See? Not too much, not too little. Just right."

"It's good," said Nat. "Now let's see you cry."

Alex spun around. "It's *good*? That's all you can say about it? It's much nicer than your stupid rock star look."

"My rock-star look is cool," said Nat. "Girls think so."

"This?" Alex made a goofy face and pretended to adjust his hair, in the mirror.

"Not that," said Nat. "This." He looked into the mirror, puckered his lips, and sucked in his cheeks. He pretended to adjust his hair, too, but in a much cooler way.

Alex rolled his eyes. "Please."

Nat moved away from the mirror. "Anyway, show me how you cry."

Alex turned his back, as if getting into character. Then he spun around. "First, let's make a bet."

"About what?" asked Nat.

"That I can get whatever I want by fake crying," he replied. "Ten bucks plus I can use your electric pencil sharpener anytime I want."

"Okay," agreed Nat. "But first show me how you do it."

Alex spread his arms. "All right, give me some space." He stepped back, took a deep breath, and buried his face in his hands. Muffled sobs echoed through the bathroom.

"That is so fake!" yelled Nat. "It doesn't count when you cover your eyes. That's cheating."

Alex scowled at him. "You interrupted me in mid-cry! I'm not going to do it now!" He turned and crossed his arms.

Nat put a hand on his shoulder. "Alex, I'm sorry. Please do it. I want to see. Really."

Alex shrugged Nat's hand away. "Forget it!" He stormed into their bedroom and slammed the door.

Nat knocked lightly. "Alex, please let me in."

"No!" yelled Alex.

Nat opened the door anyway and found Alex sitting on his bed. Tears streamed from his eyes. He didn't realize his little brother was so upset. He sat beside him. "Alex, I'm so sorry. Are you okay?"

Alex sobbed louder. "You wouldn't let me complete my demonstration," he said with a trembling lip. Tears ran down his cheeks.

"I'm sorry, man," said Nat. "I really am."

Alex looked up and smiled. "Psych!"

Nat sprung out of bed. "Whoa! Dude! That's so awesome!"

"Ten bucks," said Alex. He reached over and grabbed Nat's electric pencil sharpener. "Plus, anytime pencil sharpener usage."

Nat frowned. "You abuse that thing, man. You use it on pencils that are already sharp."

Alex smiled. "I love how it feels sawing them up and making them pointy."

Nat sighed. "Okay, just please don't do it when I'm sleeping, the way you always do."

Alex turned the sharpener over in his hands. "The deal was for *anytime* sharpener usage."

"All right," said Nat. He sat back down by his brother. "Wow, real tears. I'm impressed. How do you do it?"

Alex shrugged. "I'm a deep guy."

The next day, the cameras set up in the second sound stage. The entire space was filled with a large green screen. The screen gently curved down from the wall and onto the floor. It was used when they wanted to create a special effect. With a green screen, they could videotape someone standing in front of it and then, using a computer, make it look like they were standing anywhere. They could be in a city, on the moon, or even on an island. For the music video, they would look as if they were standing in the middle of the desert.

Nat and Rosalina were back in costume and stood on the screen while the crew made the final adjustments. Nat's turban was the same color as before but the rest of his costume was now green to match the background. He even wore green gloves and boots.

The director walked onto the set, took one look at Nat's new costume, then yelled. "Costumer!"

Ginger, the wardrobe lady ran over to the director looking a bit frazzled; some strands of her auburn hair had fallen from her ponytail.

The director pointed to his video monitor. "My darling, will you see what you have done?" he asked. "This is called a green screen. It is a magical thing we use to make magical things disappear on the camera."

Nat looked at his own monitor to see himself and Rosalina standing on all green.

"Right now you have dressed the genie all in green," said the director. "Now he will be only a genie head." He flicked a switch and the green was replaced with the desert scene. Nat's body disappeared as well. His head seemed to magically float beside Rosalina.

"I thought you asked me to," said Ginger.

"No, no, no!" The director took off his glasses and massaged his temples. "I asked you to make the bottoms of his legs disappear so he can whoosh in and out of his lamp, not to disappear his entire body." He tapped on the video screen. "Do you think the beautiful princess will be in love with a genie head?"

"That would be pretty creepy," said Rosalina.

Nat laughed. "You'd dump me for a little problem like that?" he asked. "Just because I only have a head?"

Rosalina giggled. "Yep."

"I'm a genie. I can grant you any wish you want," said Nat. "You can wish for me to have a body."

Rosalina shook her head. "Nope. I'll save my three wishes for more important things."

The director strode onto the green screen and ushered Nat toward the door. "Hey, genie head, go change. Move, move!"

Nat looked back at Rosalina and smiled. "You're very cold, Arabian princess. Watch out or the genie head won't grant you any wishes at all." She laughed as he left the sound stage.

Nat passed by the lounge and saw Alex. He sat in one of the school desks with Nat's electric pencil sharpener and dozens of pencils. He happily ground pencil after pencil into sharp points. Nat went inside and plopped down in a desk beside him.

"Is it St. Patrick's Day?" asked Alex.

"No. I have to change," said Nat. He untied the sash from around his waste. "The evil neck-biter from Transylvania says I'm too green."

"He's right for once," said Alex.

"Hey Alex, it's so cool. When Rosalina and I are in our costumes, we have the best conversations," said Nat. "I say so many funny things, like: *Watch out or the genie head won't grant you any wishes*. Stuff like that."

Alex rolled his eyes. "She must be enchanted."

"If you'd been there you would have seen how great our conversations went," said Nat. "Like they have in movies."

"Cool," said Alex. He sharpened another pencil. "Remember the bet? You owe me ten more bucks."

"No way!" yelled Nat. "What happened?"

Alex shrugged. "I cried and I got what I wanted. Pay up."

Nat sighed. "Who?"

"Jesse," replied Alex.

"What did she give you?" asked Nat.

Alex grinned. "Unlimited TV watching privileges."

"What? I don't believe you," said Nat.

Alex grabbed another pencil. "Ask her."

"How did you do it?" asked Nat.

"It's hard to remember, I get caught up in the moment." He felt the pencil's sharp point with this thumb.

"But are you faking or are you really feeling it?" asked Nat. He had to learn Alex's secret.

"I'm really feeling it," said Alex.

"You're really feeling what?" asked Nat.

"I'm really feeling the fake feelings," said Alex. The sharpener whirred as another pencil was ground down.

"But how do you get the tears to actually pour out of your eyes?" asked Nat.

"I told you," said Alex. "I'm deep."

Once Nat was in the correct wardrobe, they finished shooting the rest of the green-screen scenes. After Nat video-taped some scenes by himself, he was the last to leave. Jesse hung around to walk him home. As they left the studio and walked down the sidewalk, Nat's curiosity couldn't take it any longer.

"Did you really let Alex have unlimited TV privileges?" he asked.

"Oh, yes," she replied. "You should have seen him. I've never seen Alex so upset."

"Jesse, I swear to you he was faking," Nat explained. "He fooled me too. He can fake *real* feelings."

"Fake real feelings?" asked Jesse. "That's like, you know . . . what's that word?"

"Antihistamine?" he asked.

"Is that the word?" asked Jesse.

"I don't know," replied Nat. "It was the first word that popped into my head."

Jesse shook her head. "Anyway, you should be nicer to your brother. He's suffering so much."

Nat moaned. "Jesse, he's doing it to win a bet with me."

"I've never seen this insensitive side of you before," said Jesse. "I'm telling you, I was there. I know Alex and that poor little boy was crying his eyes out. Real tears."

"What did he say?" asked Nat.

Jesse waved a hand in front of her face. Her eyes filled with tears as well. "Oh, I was almost crying myself." She took a breath and pulled herself together. "He told me that none of his little friends would play with him because he wasn't up to date with all the television shows they watched."

"What?" asked Nat.

"He said he was an outcast," she continued. "Left alone in the playground with a carton of milk and a lonely soul."

"He actually said that?" Nat smiled. "Wow, a carton of milk and a lonely soul. He earned those ten bucks."

Jesse stopped and knelt in front of Nat. "I think you might be jealous of your brother's openness of feeling. Do you think that might be possible?"

"Definitely," he replied. He had to cry real tears soon. He had to figure out how to be as deep as Alex.

She dug through her purse. "Nat, I want you to watch these sensitivity training videos." She pulled out two DVDs and gave them to him. "I think you need to open yourself up to love and trust."

That night, Nat sat through two painfully boring sensitivity videos with Alex and their dad. The videos were filled with images of puppies, flowers, and babbling brooks. All the while, the sensitivity trainer's calm voice prompted the viewer to repeat sensitive phrases. Nat didn't see what the big deal was. However, his dad and brother sat beside him, bawling their eyes out.

"I just want to feel safe to open my heart to you," said the trainer.

"I just want to feel safe to open my heart to you," repeated Alex and their dad.

"I want to be surrounded by trust," said the trainer.

His brother and father sobbed harder. "I want to be surrounded by trust."

"I want to be embraced by your generosity," said the trainer.

The two embraced in a hug. "I want to be embraced by your generosity." They cried harder. Nat simply yawned.

"Dad, can I have a new skateboard?" Alex asked between sobs.

"Of course you can," said his dad. He hugged him tighter.

Nat couldn't believe his ears. "What?"

Alex smiled at Nat over their dad's shoulder. He mouthed, *ten more bucks* and pretended to run a pencil through the sharpener. Oblivious, their dad cried harder.

The next morning, as Nat arrived at the studio, he bumped into Rosalina in front of the hair and make-up room.

"Hi," said Rosalina.

Nat waved. "Hi."

"I haven't seen you without the genie costume for awhile," she said.

"The genie costume?" he asked. His stomach felt fluttery. His confidence was gone. "Oh, right. Yeah." He had trouble thinking of what to say. "Or you without your . . . princess thing."

"Right," she said. They shared an awkward silence. Finally, she waved again. "Okay. See you on the set."

"Right," said Nat. Embarrassed, he shoved his hands into his pockets and began to walk away.

"Nat," Rosalina called after him.

He spun around. "Yeah?"

"I don't know if I told you before but I really love this song we're doing," she said. "It's so . . . mysterious and emotional."

Nat tried to think of a cool reply. "Emotional? I wrote it in history class when I was bored." Unfortunately, that wasn't a cool reply at all.

"Oh," said Rosalina. "Well, I really like it." She waved again. "Okay, see you." She ducked back into the make-up room.

Nat tromped down the hallway. *Idiot!* he told himself. *You're the stupidest person in the world! Why did you say that?* For the past two days, he and Rosalina had fun conversations. There weren't any awkward pauses and he didn't say stupid things at the worst possible moments — like when the girl he likes pays him a compliment. Why couldn't he talk to her? He looked down at his jeans and shirt and groaned. He figured it out.

Cooper turned down the hall. "What's the matter, Nat?"

"You know what the matter is?" asked Nat. "I'm not wearing my costume. That's what the matter is." He marched toward his dressing room. "When I'm wearing my costume I say the right things to Rosalina, and when I'm not, I don't. It's as simple as that!"

Cooper followed him inside. "What did you say to her?"

"I told her I wrote my song in history class," he replied. He took off his shirt and put on his genie shirt.

"So, she thinks you should study harder at history?" asked Cooper.

"No! I just made it sound like I whipped up that song without feeling anything," replied Nat. "Like I'm not a deep guy. I'm a deep guy, right?"

"Yeah, definitely," replied Cooper. "You're deep."

Nat pulled his genie pants over his jeans. "Girls like deep guys."

"That's true," said Cooper.

Nat tied the sash around his waist. "Alex is a deep guy."

"Alex?" asked Cooper.

"You should see him," said Nat. "He's like a black-belt crier. He gets everything he wants."

Cooper frowned. "That doesn't make him deep. That just makes him a good faker."

"I know," said Nat. "But nobody knows the difference." He tucked in his shirt and put on his vest. "If Rosalina had told him his song was emotional and mysterious he would've cried and told her about his carton of milk and his lonely soul."

"Lonely soul?" asked Cooper. "That's a good one."

Nat placed his genie turban onto his head. "Okay. I've got my costume on. I can talk to her now without making a fool of myself." He pointed to the door. "Look outside. Check and see if she's coming."

Cooper opened the door and poked his head out. He ducked back in. "She's coming."

Nat leaped through the doorway as Rosalina walked by. "All hail, the Arabian princess!"

She gave him a confused look. "Should we be in our costumes now?"

"Uh, no," he replied. "I . . . uh . . ." He still couldn't think of anything to say. He decided to fall back on one of the previous costumed conversations. "I . . . just wanted to grant a few wishes. Talk about deep things . . . like my song."

"Your song?" asked Rosalina.

"Yeah, my song," he replied. "It meant a lot to me that you found it emotional. In fact, I was quite emotional when I wrote it." He made his lip quiver.

"You were?" asked Rosalina.

"Yes," he replied. He scrunched up his face and pretended to cry.

Rosalina smiled. "Nat?"

"Yes?" he asked through fake sobs.

"Are you laughing?"

Nat's eyes widened. "Uh, yeah." He laughed nervously. He stared at her for a moment. His mind went completely blank. Finally, he gave up. "See ya." He ducked back into his dressing room and closed the door.

"Well?" asked Cooper.

Nat threw his turban across the room. "I'm still an idiot."

Nat changed back into his street clothes. He and Cooper left the dressing room and ambled down the hallway. "The costume doesn't work, and I am the worst crier in the world," said Nat. "I couldn't squeeze out one tear."

"Have you tried pulling out a nose hair?" Cooper suggested.

"Pulling out a nose hair?"

"Yeah, I've seen my mom do it," said Cooper. "I guess it hurts so much that it makes you cry."

"Why would your mom want to do it in the first place?" asked Nat.

"Ladies don't like unwanted hair," he replied.

"Do kids even have unwanted hair?" asked Nat.

"I don't know." He grabbed Nat by the shoulders and peered up his nose. "I don't see any. See if you can feel any."

"You mean stick my finger up my nose?" asked Nat.

"Sure," said Cooper.

"Okay." Nat shoved his index finger into one nostril. He felt around for nose hairs.

"You feel any?" asked Cooper.

"Not yet," said Nat.

Just then, they turned a corner and there stood Rosalina. Her and Nat's eyes locked as she took a sip from a bottle of juice. Her eyes widened, and she almost choked on her drink in surprise.

Nat shot his hand down to his side and briskly walked away from her. Cooper shuffled to keep up. When they were far enough away, Nat spun and grabbed Cooper's shoulders. "She thinks I was picking my nose!"

"Sorry," said Cooper.

Nat groaned. "She thinks I'm one of those nose-picking kind of guys."

"But you're not a nose-picking kind of guy," Cooper assured him.

"Now Rosalina thinks I am!" shouted Nat. "She thinks I'm an insensitive, shallow, fake-crying nose picker!"

Cooper shrugged. "I don't know what to say."

Jesse turned the corner. "Hey, Nat! How did those sensitivity tapes work out for you?"

"Great," he replied. "Alex got a new skateboard."

Jesse gasped. "Oh, I'm so glad. That's the sweet, generous-spirited Nat I know!"

As she trotted away, Alex rolled around the corner on his new skateboard. He skipped it off the ground and laughed. "I can't believe how well I can ollie on this thing!"

Nat growled as he watched him skate away. "I'm going to kill him."

As he and Cooper walked into the sound stage, they spotted Thomas, David, and Qaasim standing around the craft service table. It was a table covered in snacks for the cast and crew. The strange thing was that all three boys had tears streaming down their cheeks.

Nat ran up to them. "Are you guys crying?"

"No," said Thomas in a hoarse voice. "We're eating hot sauce from these packets." A mound of empty sauce packets covered the table.

"Qaasim ate five packets all at once," said David. He gave Qaasim a high five. "You rule, man!"

Thomas held a handful of open packets up to his mouth. "Six! Check it out!" He squeezed them into his mouth. More tears streamed from his eyes as he gasped for air.

"Thomas, your eyes are bugging out," said Qaasim.

Thomas raised a triumphant fist. "I win. I win!" He coughed and then rummaged through a nearby ice chest. "I need water!"

Nat couldn't believe how easily they were crying. And with just a little thing like hot sauce. "Wow, look at those tears." He grabbed a handful of packets. "Give me some of those."

Cooper followed Nat as he headed for the exit. One by one, Nat tore open ten of the hot sauce packets. "I need to show her I can be emotional," he said. "If she sees real tears coming down my face she'll comfort me and think I'm deep."

"And how do we solve the nose picking problem?" asked Cooper.

Nat shook his head. "Let's just take this one step at a time."

Cooper elbowed him. "She's coming." Rosalina entered the stage and walked toward them.

"Comfort me," said Nat. He squeezed out the contents of all ten sauce packets into his mouth.

Suddenly, Nat's mouth was on fire. His throat tightened and he couldn't breath. Nat grabbed his throat and coughed. By the time Rosalina approached, it looked like he was choking to death instead of crying.

"Is he okay?" asked Rosalina.

"Yeah, just emotional," Cooper replied. He gently pat Nat on the back. "There, there, Nat. It's only a song."

"Cooper, I think he needs the Heimlich maneuver," said Rosalina.

Nat dropped to his knees and struggled to breath. This was not the effect he was going for.

15

Once the paramedics had left, Nat changed back into his genie costume. He was still a bit woozy, but he felt he could go on with the video shoot. He walked back into the sound stage. The rest of the band was already there and in costume. Rosalina was the first to come up to him.

"You okay, Nat?" she asked.

"Yeah, I'm fine now," said Nat.

The others gathered around him. "That was so cool having those paramedics come and pump your stomach," said Thomas.

"Yeah, that was so gross," said David. "Do you think that's going to be in all the papers tomorrow?"

Nat's stomach tightened again. "Can we not talk about it?"

"Sure, Nat," said Qaasim. "We're just glad you're feeling better, man."

Everyone went back to the set. Nat was embarrassed and tired — and his stomach was sore. He just wanted to finish shooting and go home.

Cooper came up and whispered in his ear. "The good news is, after what just happened, I don't think Rosalina remembers you picking your nose anymore."

"I didn't pick my nose!" yelled Nat. The sound stage fell silent and everyone stared at him, including Rosalina.

"I think you just refreshed her memory," Cooper said as he slowly backed away.

The director marched into the room. "Okay, so now, we have the big wedding of beautiful Arabian princess and evil sultan," he shouted and clapped his hands. "Think Obelisk, everyone. Obelisk!"

Nat, Alex, and Rosalina took their places to rehearse the scene. The director had Rosalina put her hands on Alex's shoulders. He crossed his arms and frowned, playing the evil sultan all the way. Then the director motioned for her to move to Nat. "The princess really wants to be with the genie," he said.

Nat took her hand and dramatically twirled her into his arms. When she was close, he whispered into her ear. "I never pick my nose."

"What?" asked Rosalina.

"But that means living forever with him in his lamp," said the director. "And she knows that would be no life for her." The director moved her back to Alex. "So she is resigned to live with the sultan. A man she does not love."

Alex burst into tears. "That's not very nice. Why don't you love me?" He sobbed louder. "I'll give you a happy life with lots of riches . . . and grapes."

Nat couldn't believe he was doing this.

"You poor little sweetie," said Rosalina, hugging him. "Of course I love you. I love you more than that silly old genie in his smelly old lamp."

Alex poured it on. He seemed to be going above and beyond his character of the sultan. So much so, that the rest of the band embraced him as he cried.

Nat shook his head. "I can't believe this is happening."

Alex poked his head out from the mass of comforting arms. He grinned at Nat. "Ten more bucks," he whispered.

The director clapped his hands again. "All right. Enough of the funny business." He put everyone back in their original positions. After they rehearsed a few more times, they were ready to shoot the scene.

"And . . . actions!" yelled the director. The music played back and the cameras moved in. Nat, Alex, and Rosalina went through all the moves. They hit their marks perfectly. Finally, at the end of the scene, it was Nat's big moment.

"Okay, genie. You've lost your love," said the director. "Now, cry!"

Nat did his best but nothing happened. He thought back to the sensitivity videos, but he didn't feel anything. He didn't have a nose hair to pull either. Even after eating all that hot sauce, he still didn't cry. He just couldn't do it.

Nat waved his hands. "Cut!"

The director turned to Cooper. "Did he just say *cut*?"

"I think so," Cooper replied.

He stormed onto the set. "But I'm the director! I am the only one who can say *cut*!"

"Sorry everybody, I can't do this," said Nat. He turned to the director. "I'm sorry about your Obelisk award. I know you wanted to win it for this video. I just can't cry. I've tried everything so don't waste your time with me. I have no emotions. I'm not deep. I have no talent."

The director smiled. "Of course you don't. This is why I bring my special acting tears."

"Acting tears?" asked Nat.

"Yes, of course, all actors use them," said the director. "You think Vaclav Kleimanspiel has talent? No. He has acting tears."

"Who's Vacuum Climbingspoon?" asked Qaasim.

"Vaclav Kleimanspiel!" the director corrected. "The greatest actor in the world. From my country, of course."

Qaasim leaned closer to David and whispered, "Where is his country?"

"No one knows," David replied.

"What do you do with these acting tears?" asked Nat.

"You put them in your eyes and poof, you cry like a baby," the director explained.

"Amazing!" said Nat. Waves of relief washed over him. His problems were over. So what if he wasn't deep like Alex. He still had tons of other good qualities. He was a good, caring friend. He was a loving brother. He didn't have to cry on demand to prove anything.

"Here, we do it now," said the director. He snapped his fingers. "Costumer!"

Ginger shuffled over and dug out a small plastic vial from her pocket. It looked like an ordinary bottle of eye drops. She handed it to the director. He took off the cap, tilted Nat's head back, and squeezed the vial over one eye. Nothing happened.

"What happened to my acting tears?" he asked Ginger. "Why the bottle is empty?"

"I'm so sorry, sir," she replied. "Alex has been borrowing them."

"What?!" roared Nat. He rounded on Alex. "You're a deep guy?! You get caught up in the moment?!"

"Oh, poopoosauce," said Alex. He ran across the set.

"Give me back my money!" yelled Nat. He chased Alex through the tent.

"Help! Help!" yelled Alex as he ducked around the curtains on the set.

"Give me my pencil sharpener!" yelled Nat as he hopped over satin pillows.

"I will! I will!" shouted Alex. "Please don't kill me!"

Alex pushed by the table of fake fruit. As Nat gave chase, the large bowl of cement grapes toppled off and landed on his foot. "Owwww!" screamed Nat. Pain exploded and shot up his leg. He fell to the ground and held his hurt foot. The pain was so intense, he began to cry.

"Camera, push in," ordered the director. "This is Obelisk moment . . ."

The camera moved closer to Nat as tears streamed down his face. So what if it took a bowl full of cement grapes crushing his toes to make him cry? At least they got the shot. He didn't know if this music video would win another VMA or even an Obelisk, but he certainly gave it his all. Never let it be said that Nat Wolff didn't suffer for his art.

Then again, what rock star didn't?

We won! We won! We totally won! We won the VMA for Best Music Video!

Woohoo!!!!!

I knew we would! Well, I sorta knew we would. OK, so Nat and I were a little nervous. But we had hope—even though Matt Pinfield predicted that we were going down.

But what little hope we had was gone once Jesse read us our horoscopes (more like horror-scopes). Jesse said that horoscopes are so accurate they're scary. And she wasn't kidding, because what she said scared the heck out of me.

First she told us this super creepy story about her friend who *died* of food poisoning at Clam's Casino all because his horoscope predicted it. Yeah, you heard right: DIED! Then she told Nat that if he failed he would take everyone else down with him. So Nat's horoscope was bad, but his was nothing compared to mine, which basically said: If you don't get crushed by a large falling object first, you will most definitely get into a massive car crash. And really, you should just stay in your PJ's and not leave your bed today at all because if you do, you're toast.

Sheesh.

Just what a kid wants to hear on the most important day of his eight-year-old life! I wasn't planning to go the way of the Clam's Casino guy, no way Jose. So I needed to seriously focus on being ware. You know, like the horoscope said: Be ware.

What else could I do? I strapped a pillow on my head and tried to avoid falling objects and motor vehicles at all costs. It was rough, trust me. (Have you ever tried to keep rhythm with a giant fluffy object tied to your head? Not easy.) And it didn't help that Thomas and David were up to their old tricks. (They thought it'd be funny to drop a bucket of water on my head. They're so immature.) But, it's cool. I got them back. No one out-pranks Alex Wolff. (Never underestimate the power of a little carefully placed Hot Ice Vapor Rub.)

Anyway, despite my horoscope of doom, we ended up getting to the VMAs in style. Since there was no way I was stepping foot into the limo, we got a ride on this crazy bicycle built for six. It was awesome! But not nearly as awesome as the VMAs were because we totally WON! (Take that, Pinfield!)

Ahh, victory is so sweet - even when your dad almost ruins it by playing his accordion onstage. Oh well, you can't win them all, I guess!

So I learned something very important about horoscopes today: Don't ever
read them! Especially on award show
days!

Later skaters,
Alex .

Acting tears. Ever heard of 'em? I hadn't either until yesterday, but I wish I'd known about them a long time ago. (They should really advertise!)

It all started when our crazy director wanted me to cry in our video for "Sometimes I'll Be There." (Why exactly I had to cry, I'm not sure, but it has something to do with winning an Obelisk, which is some sort of Transylvanian video-music award or something.) Anyway, I was totally stoked about the video because Rosalina and I got to dress up in these really cool costumes. She was an Arabian princess, and I got to be a genie. And the best part was that when we were in costume, it was like I said the funniest stuff ever.

So the video was gonna be totally cool, except that my fake crying well, it kinda stinks. Seriously, when I try to cry, it looks like I swallowed a bumble bee and I'm squinching up my face all weird and trying not to laugh. It's pretty embarrassing.

But the crying thing was about more than just doing the video, it was about showing Rosalina how deep and emotional I was. I mean, that's totally what girls dig, right? Deep, emotional guys.

So I asked Alex for help (that was my first mistake). He fooled me into believing that he was an expert fake-crier. Seriously, he just had to think about crying and - boom! Tears! Just like that. He made it look sooo easy. So we made a bet: If he could get whatever he wanted by fake crying, I'd give him $10 bucks each time *plus* unlimited use of my electric pencil sharpener. (Don't ask me about the pencil sharpener thing, I don't get it either.)

The bet was on, and I watched in horror as Alex cried his way into getting WHATEVER he wanted. It was insane: unlimited TV-watching privileges from Jesse *and* a brand-new skateboard from Dad. WHAT?!

I was getting desperate. I *had* to fake cry somehow. Now, I'm not proud about what I'm about to tell you, but remember, I was feeling trapped. So when Cooper told me to try pulling out a nose-hair, I was game. At that point, I would have done anything to drop a few tears. Unfortunately, who should happen to walk by at the very moment when I had my finger crammed halfway up my nostril? (I'll give you one guess.) Yup, the beautiful Arabian princess herself, Rosalina.

So not only was I a shallow, unemotional fake-crying failure, but I was also a nose-picker! Things were going from bad to worse, and when we were re-shooting the video, I lost it when it came time for the waterworks to begin.

"Cut!"

I had to come clean. I couldn't fake cry! But apparently, spooky Transylvanian directors are good for one thing: providing special acting tears. But when Dracula tested out the tears, the whole bottle was empty. It seems a certain *someone* had been using them all week. And I wonder who that someone could be...you guessed it: my dear little brother Alex.

Turns out that with the help of acting tears, anyone can be a deep, emotional person. But come on... Alex? Emotional? We all should've known better.

P.S. That reminds me: Alex, you owe me $30 bucks, bro! Pay up!

Well, gotta run, band rehearsal. Rock on dudes and thanks for reading!

Nat

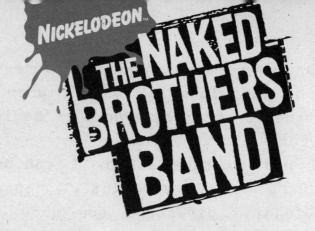

ROCK 'N' READ!

Can't get enough of the Naked Brothers Band? Well, then check out all these new books. Get ready. Get set. Get rockin'!

0-545-02071-9 The Making of the Naked Brothers Band Scrapbook
Get the scoop on the Naked Brothers Band with this scrapbook featuring lots of photos and tons of behind the scenes info!

0-545-02072-7 The Naked Brothers Band Poster Song Book
Learn the lyrics to all your favorite NBB songs! Filled with pictures of the band and lyrics to their songs, this is the only way to sing along with the hottest group around.

0-545-03921-5 Naked Brothers Band: Chapter Book #2 Battle of the Bands
It's East Coast versus West Coast when Bobby Love and the L.A. Surfers roll into town. After Nat learns Bobby Love's true identity, things start getting ugly. The Naked Brothers Band and the Surfers clash as a charity even they play turns into an all-out war . . . . Nat knows the truth, but when Rosalina falls head over heels for Bobby, things go from bad to worse. Who will come out on top?

. . . And stay tuned for more to come!